Dear Parent:
Your child's love of reading starts here!

Every child learns to read in a different way and at his or her own speed. Some go back and forth between reading levels and read favorite books again and again. Others read through each level in order. You can help your young reader improve and become more confident by encouraging his or her own interests and abilities. From books your child reads with you to the first books he or she reads alone, there are I Can Read Books for every stage of reading:

SHARED READING
Basic language, word repetition, and whimsical illustrations, ideal for sharing with your emergent reader

BEGINNING READING
Short sentences, familiar words, and simple concepts for children eager to read on their own

READING WITH HELP
Engaging stories, longer sentences, and language play for developing readers

READING ALONE
Complex plots, challenging vocabulary, and high-interest topics for the independent reader

ADVANCED READING
Short paragraphs, chapters, and exciting themes for the perfect bridge to chapter books

By Poop head

I Can Read Books have introduced children to the joy of reading since 1957. Featuring award-winning authors and illustrators and a fabulous cast of beloved characters, I Can Read Books set the standard for beginning readers.

A lifetime of discovery begins with the magical words **"I Can Read!"**

Visit www.icanread.com for information
on enriching your child's reading experience.

Marley: Farm Dog Copyright © 2011 by John Grogan All rights reserved. Manufactured in China. No part of this book may be used or reproduced in any manner whatsoever without written permission except in the case of brief quotations embodied in critical articles and reviews. For information address HarperCollins Children's Books, a division of HarperCollins Publishers, 10 East 53rd Street, New York, NY 10022.
www.icanread.com

Library of Congress catalog card number: 2010920048
ISBN 978-0-06-198938-4 (trade bdg.)—ISBN 978-0-06-198937-7 (pbk.)

11 12 13 14 15   SCP   10 9 8 7 6 5 4 3 2 1   ❖   First Edition

Marley

FARM DOG

**BASED ON THE BESTSELLING
BOOKS BY JOHN GROGAN**

COVER ART BY RICHARD COWDREY

TEXT BY SUSAN HILL

INTERIOR ILLUSTRATIONS BY LYDIA HALVERSON

HARPER

An Imprint of HarperCollinsPublishers

Cassie and her family were
going to visit Uncle Bob's farm.
Daddy smiled at Cassie.
"Marley is even more excited
than you are," he said.

Uncle Bob waved

and opened Cassie's door.

Marley jumped out of the car.

Then he jumped into the pond.

"Look!" said Cassie.

"Marley's doing the dog paddle!"

Uncle Bob laughed.

"It's fine for Marley to play,

but we need to get to work!

Will you be my helper, Cassie?"

asked Uncle Bob.

"Yes, please!" said Cassie.

Cassie helped with lots of chores.

She worked in the dirt,

planting and watering.

Every time Uncle Bob gave Cassie

a new chore to do,

Cassie said, "I can help!"

Marley tried to help, too.

Then Uncle Bob showed Cassie the barn.

It was full of big, gentle cows.

Uncle Bob brought out a tiny calf.

"This calf needs extra help

in order to eat," Uncle Bob said.

"I can help," Cassie said.

Uncle Bob gave Cassie

a bottle full of milk.

Then Cassie sat down

next to the calf.

The calf began to drink the milk.

"Look, Marley!" Cassie said.

"He likes it!"

"Time to put the other animals back in their houses," said Uncle Bob.

"I can help!" thought Marley.

Marley ran around and around
the chickens.

The chickens ran around and around
the yard.

Then Marley tried to herd the sheep.
The sheep leaped and jumped
and played.

"Marley isn't a very good sheepdog,"
said Cassie.

Cassie and Marley helped Uncle Bob
put the chickens into the chicken coop.
They helped put the sheep
and the lambs into their pens.
But wait!
One lamb was missing.

Cassie was worried.

"Where could the little guy be?"

she said.

"We have to find him!"

"I can help!" thought Marley.

Marley ran back to the meadow

to look for the little lamb.

At last, Marley found the lamb.

It had been fast asleep.

"There you are!" Cassie called.

The lamb was startled.

It jumped up and ran away!

Marley thought fast.

He ran to the barn.

"What are you doing, Marley?"

Cassie shouted.

"You'll see,"

Marley thought.

Marley ran back to the meadow

with a bottle of milk in his teeth.

He found the lamb

and led the little guy back home.

Now the work was over.

Uncle Bob took everyone

on a hayride.

"I didn't think Marley
was much of a sheepdog,"
said Uncle Bob.
"But I was wrong."
"You're a hero, Marley!"
said Cassie.

Then it was time to go home.

Uncle Bob thanked Cassie

for all her help on the farm.

"And thanks to Marley, too,"

he said.

"But where is Marley?" asked Daddy.

Cassie smiled.

"Maybe you are part sheepdog after all, Marley," she whispered.